GOLDILO

AND THE THREE BEARS

Illustrations by Gabhor Utomo

KENNEBUNKPORT, MAINE

13-Digit ISBN: 978-1-64643-185-4
10-Digit ISBN: 1-64643-185-5

This book may be ordered by mail from the publisher.
Please include $5.95 for postage and handling.
Please support your local bookseller first!

Books published by Cider Mill Press Book Publishers are available at special discounts for
bulk purchases in the United States by corporations, institutions, and other organizations.
For more information, please contact the publisher.

Applesauce Press is an imprint of
Cider Mill Press Book Publishers
"Where Good Books Are Ready for Press"
PO Box 454
12 Spring Street
Kennebunkport, Maine 04046

Visit us online!
cidermillpress.com

Typography: ITC Caslon 224
Printed in China

1 2 3 4 5 6 7 8 9 0
First Edition

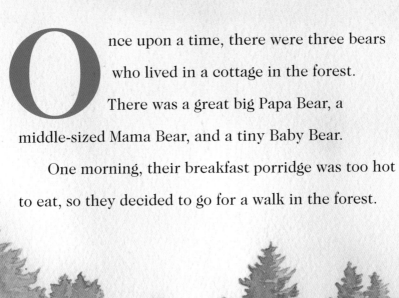

Once upon a time, there were three bears who lived in a cottage in the forest. There was a great big Papa Bear, a middle-sized Mama Bear, and a tiny Baby Bear.

One morning, their breakfast porridge was too hot to eat, so they decided to go for a walk in the forest.

On the edge of the forest lived a little girl named Goldilocks. She was called Goldilocks because her beautiful hair glistened in the sun like gold. On this day, while the bears were out, Goldilocks came through the trees and found the bears' cottage.

She peeked through the windows and didn't see
anyone inside. Then she knocked on the door, and
there was no answer. So Goldilocks pushed the door
open and went inside.

Inside she found a table with three chairs—one large chair, one middle-sized chair, and one small chair. On the table were three spoons and three bowls of porridge—one large bowl, one middle-sized bowl, and one small bowl.

Goldilocks was very hungry, and the porridge looked
delicious, so she sat in the largest chair and picked up the largest
spoon. The chair was very big and very hard, and the spoon was
very heavy. She tried some of the porridge from the big bowl.

"Ouch! This porridge is too hot!" she cried.

Goldilocks quickly jumped off the seat and went over to the middle-sized chair. This chair was far too soft. Next, she tried the porridge from the middle-sized bowl.

"This porridge is too cold!" she said.

So she went over to the little chair, picked up the smallest spoon, and tried some of the porridge from the tiny bowl. This time it was neither too hot nor too cold. It was just right. It was so delicious that she ate it all up. But she was too heavy for the little chair, and just as she finished eating, it broke into pieces under her weight.

Next, Goldilocks went upstairs, where she found three beds. There was a great big bed, a middle-sized bed, and a tiny bed. By now she was feeling very sleepy, so she climbed into the big bed and laid down. But she found it was not comfortable at all.

"This bed is very hard and far too big!" she cried.

Then she tried the middle-sized bed. "This bed is far too soft!"

At last, she climbed into the smallest bed. It was neither too hard nor too soft. In fact, it felt just right. She pulled the covers up, and in no time at all Goldilocks was fast asleep.

While she was sleeping, the three bears came back from their walk in the forest. They saw the open door at once. Papa Bear looked around then roared in a growly voice, "SOMEBODY HAS BEEN SITTING IN MY CHAIR!"

Mama Bear said in a quiet, gentle voice, "Somebody has been sitting in my chair."

Then Baby Bear cried in a small, squeaky voice, "Somebody has been sitting in my chair and has broken it!"

Then Papa Bear looked at his bowl of porridge and saw the spoon in it. He said in his great big voice, "SOMEBODY HAS BEEN EATING MY PORRIDGE!"

Then Mama Bear saw that her bowl had a spoon in it and said in her quiet voice, "Somebody has been eating my porridge."

Baby Bear looked at his porridge bowl and cried in his small, squeaky voice, "Somebody has been eating my porridge and has eaten it all up!"

Then the three bears went upstairs, and Papa Bear saw at once that his bed was untidy. He growled in his great big voice, "SOMEBODY HAS BEEN SLEEPING IN MY BED!"

Mama Bear saw that her bed had the bedclothes turned back, and she said in her quiet, gentle voice, "Somebody has been sleeping in my bed."

Then Baby Bear looked at his bed and saw a little girl with golden curls snoring away on his pillow, fast asleep. In his small, squeaky voice, Baby Bear cried, "Somebody is sleeping in my bed!"

He squeaked so loudly that Goldilocks woke up with a start. "Help!" she cried. Frightened, she jumped out of bed and away she ran, down the stairs and out into the forest. The three bears never saw her again.